P9-DDX-755

GHOST DETECTORS

Lions, Tiger & Bears, Oh My!

BOOK 24

BY
JAN FIELDS

ILLUSTRATED BY
DAVE SHEPHARD

Calico

An Imprint of Magic Wagon
abdopublishing.com

For all the fantastic people who edit my work and make me look so good. — JF

For my dear old sisters. When I grow up I'd like to be just like you. — DS

abdopublishing.com

Published by Magic Wagon, a division of ABDO, PO Box 398166, Minneapolis, Minnesota 55439. Copyright © 2018 by Abdo Consulting Group, Inc. International copyrights reserved in all countries. No part of this book may be reproduced in any form without written permission from the publisher. Calico™ is a trademark and logo of Magic Wagon.

Printed in the United States of America, North Mankato, Minnesota.
102017
012018

THIS BOOK CONTAINS
RECYCLED MATERIALS

Written by Jan Fields
Illustrated by Dave Shephard
Edited by Bridget O'Brien
Designed by Christina Doffing

Publisher's Cataloging-in-Publication Data

Names: Fields, Jan, author. | Shephard, Dave, illustrator.
Title: Lions, tiger & bears, oh my! / by Jan Fields; illustrated by Dave
    Shephard.
Description: Minneapolis, Minnesota : Magic Wagon, 2018. |
    Series: Ghost detectors; Book 24
Summary: A field trip to the zoo goes bananas when animals break
    out of their cages and Malcolm is banned from the park, so the boys
    enlist Mrs. Goolsby's help to zap the ghost setting the animals free.
Identifiers: LCCN 2017946560 | ISBN 9781532131561 (lib.bdg.) | ISBN
    9781532131660 (ebook) | ISBN 9781532131714 (Read-to-me ebook)
Subjects: LCSH: Ghost stories--Juvenile fiction. | Zoos--Juvenile fiction.
    | Zoo animals--Juvenile fiction. | Humorous Stories--Juvenile fiction.
Classification: DDC [FIC]--dc23
LC record available at https://lccn.loc.gov/2017946560

Contents

Chapter 1
Wild Wonders

Malcolm's legs stuck to the hot bus seat. He scrambled up on his knees to open the window. He tugged and tugged, but the window wouldn't budge. "Can you give me a hand?"

Dandy looked up from the book in his lap. He clapped his hands.

"What was that for?"

Dandy shrugged. "I don't know. My dad always does that when I ask him to give me a hand. It's supposed to be funny."

Malcolm groaned. "Really? We're doing dad jokes now?"

"You can't argue with a classic." Dandy flipped a page. "Dad says that too."

"Malcolm," Mrs. Goolsby called from her seat. "Please sit down. It's time to leave."

"The window won't open," Malcolm complained. The bus driver cranked the engine and the roar drowned out Malcolm's voice. With a sigh, he slid back down the hot seat. "I'm going to melt to death."

Dandy looked up from his book. "At least you're wearing shorts. My mom said shorts are an invitation to be bitten by a mosquito carrying an exotic zoo disease."

"What keeps them from biting your hands or your head?" Malcolm asked.

"Bug spray," Dandy said. "I have three cans. I can share some with you."

"Sounds great, Dandy," Malcolm muttered. "Bug spray and sweat. I'll have a slime-a-thon."

Dandy shrugged. "At least this field trip is cool." Then he laughed at his own joke.

Malcolm groaned again. But he had to admit, "The zoo is cool."

A head popped up over the seat in front of them. Big, blue eyes stared at them through round glasses. "Wild Wonderland Animal Rescue Park isn't a zoo."

Malcolm rolled his eyes. Rosie Main never missed a chance to show off. "Does it have lions?" he asked.

"Yes," she answered. "Three."

"Does it have tigers?"

"Just one."

"Does it have bears?"

"Two," Rosie said.

"Then it's a zoo."

Rosie glared at him and opened her mouth to argue.

"Rosie Main!" Mrs. Goolsby yelled. "Sit down while the bus is moving."

Rosie disappeared.

"Good," Malcolm said. "Now I can melt in peace."

"You should try thinking about something other than being hot." Dandy held up his book. "I checked out this animal book from the library. It's great."

"You gave yourself extra homework for the bus ride?" Malcolm wrinkled his nose. "Sometimes I worry about you."

"No really. Listen." Dandy placed his finger on a page and read aloud. "'A giraffe can clean its own nose and ears with its tongue.' I would love to be able to do that."

Malcolm tried to picture Dandy with a superlong tongue slurping at his own ear. He shuddered. "I prefer to leave my ears alone."

Dandy sighed. "Me too. But my mom says I have to wash them."

Dandy read more facts as the bus rumbled along to the zoo. Malcolm learned anteaters have spiny tongues. He also learned that the tongue of a blue whale weighs more than an elephant.

"Why are all your facts about tongues?" Malcolm asked.

Dandy held up his book so Malcolm could see the title *Lickity Spit*. "Besides, tongues are cool." Then he grinned again. "In fact, dogs cool down by panting with their tongues hanging out."

Dandy lolled out his tongue and panted.

Malcolm crossed his arms and watched his friend. "Are you cooling off?"

Dandy shook his head. He slurped his tongue back into his mouth. "I'm mostly getting thirsty. Do you have an extra water bottle? I didn't have room in my backpack with the bug spray."

"Sure." Malcolm leaned forward to unzip his backpack. He pushed the Ecto-Handheld-Automatic-Heat-Sensitive-Laser-Enhanced Specter Detector out of the way. His water bottle was buried under it.

Malcolm tried always to be prepared. On a hot day, you needed water. And on any day, you needed to be prepared for ghosts. Ghosts could be anywhere. He'd learned that much as a Ghost Detector.

Just as he grabbed the water bottle, the bus driver slammed on the brakes. Malcolm

lurched forward. He smacked his head on the seat ahead of him.

"Ouch!" Malcolm yelped.

"Look out, Malcolm!" Dandy said. He watched Malcolm rub the top of his head. "If only you were a giraffe, dude! You could have stuck your tongue up to pad your head."

"Good to know," Malcolm said. He handed over his water bottle. *And if my best friend wasn't so weird, I wouldn't have hit my head in the first place.*

He looked out the bus window. He saw a roller coaster towering over the trees in the distance. A piece was missing from the track. "What's that?"

Rosie Main's head poked over the seat. "That's the old Super Funtime Zoo and Theme Park. It was terrible."

"Really?" Malcolm looked at the banged up pieces of roller coaster again. But they disappeared from sight as the bus bounced along. "It looks like fun to me."

"Shows what you know," Rosie said. She stuck out her tongue and disappeared behind the seat again.

Finally the tall, arched entrance of the Wild Wonderland Animal Rescue Park appeared. Malcolm noticed it didn't have a cool roller coaster. But at least they were finally there. His day could only get better. Right?

Chapter 2
Snake!

The class formed a wobbly line in the parking lot. Mrs. Goolsby called out rules. *Stay together. Don't climb the walls. Don't feed the animals.* Malcolm half listened as he wiped sweat from his face with his sleeve.

Dandy rooted in his bag and pulled out his bug spray. He held up the bottle and pushed the button. The bug spray squirted out the back. It hit Malcolm in the face.

"Oops, sorry," Dandy said. "I was holding it backwards."

"Dandy," Mrs. Goolsby said. "Please, keep your bug spray to yourself. Your mom wrote a note for you to use it. Not your friends."

"And I didn't want any," Malcolm said. He wiped at his face with the sleeve of his shirt again.

"It was an accident," Dandy said. Then he turned to Malcolm. "But you'll be glad when you don't come down with any horrible diseases."

Mrs. Goolsby finished with her rules. Then she added one more thing. "I expect each of you to write a two-page report on what you learn today. Don't forget!"

The whole class groaned, but Mrs. Goolsby just shushed them. She yelled, "Let's go meet the animals. Stay with your buddy."

The group marched to the park entrance. A woman stood under a Wild Wonderland Animal Rescue sign. She wore a brown uniform with a patch that read WWAR.

Mrs. Goolsby walked up to her and stuck out her hand. "I'm Mrs. Goolsby. This is my class."

"Welcome!" the young woman said.

She grabbed Mrs. Goolsby's hand and shook it. "We are happy to have all of you today. As we say at WWAR, every day is a happy day! I'm Alice in Wild Wonderland!" The woman laughed at her own joke as she continued shaking Mrs. Goolsby's hand.

Mrs. Goolsby pulled her hand free. "We're looking forward to learning about the animals."

"Of course." Alice turned toward the class and launched into her speech. As she

talked, she bounced on her toes. Malcolm watched her head bob up and down, up and down.

Finally Alice stopped bouncing and started into the park. She waved at them to follow. "All of our animals are rescued from bad situations. Here they have plenty of food and lots of room. And every day is a happy day for them."

"That's why you're not a zoo!" Rosie Main shouted.

Alice beamed at her. "Yes, that's why we're not a zoo. We're a rescue park."

"Seems like a zoo to me," Malcolm muttered.

"No," Alice snapped. Her smile was gone. "There used to be a zoo near here. All the money went to silly rides for humans. The animals were miserable. That's a zoo!"

Malcolm didn't think that was fair. But he walked on ahead down the path. The park had lots of animal-shaped benches and trees.

Just inside the gates, a fountain sprayed water into the air from the trunk of an elephant statue. Mist from the falling water cooled the air near the fountain. Malcolm ran over to soak up the mist.

"Stay together," Alice said. "We're going to begin our visit in the reptile house."

The reptile house was a big, green shed. Pictures of squirming snakes and glaring lizards covered the outside.

Mrs. Goolsby froze at the door. "I'm going to stay out here, class," she said. Her voice was wobbly. "Our guide will show you the snakes. I expect you all to do everything Alice says."

"There's plenty of room," Alice said brightly. "You can come in too."

Mrs. Goolsby looked pale. "I don't think so. You go right ahead."

Alice shrugged at the frozen teacher. "Okay!" She herded the class into the dark, cool building.

After the bright glare of the sun, Malcolm was practically blind inside the shed. He stumbled around and bumped into Dandy. He knew it was Dandy from the bug spray smell.

"Don't worry," Alice said. "Your eyes will adjust. And all the exhibits are lighted. The lights help keep the reptiles warm."

"Wouldn't they be warmer if you kept them outside?" Dandy asked.

Alice smiled at him. Her white teeth almost glowed in the dark room. "That's

a good question. They would be warm outside today, but not in the winter. And we wouldn't want them slithering away."

She walked over to the first big tank. "Most of our reptiles come to us from owners who thought they would be good pets."

"Why weren't they good pets?" Dandy asked.

"Some grew too large," Alice said. "Some required special conditions to be happy. And some are venomous." She gestured to the tank. "Like our friend here. A king cobra. We call him Rex."

"Cobra!" The class rushed to the glass.

Malcolm had to jump and squeeze in to get a peek. He saw a few plants, a fake rock, a branch, and a lot of sand. What he didn't see was a snake.

"Is it a tiny cobra?" Malcolm asked.

Alice turned her smile toward him. "No. Rex is fully grown."

"He hides really well," Dandy said.

"We can't see him. Where is he? Where's the snake?" More and more questions and complaints came from the class.

Alice's smile dimmed as she turned toward the tank. "I'm certain if you look closely you'll see him." Then she stopped talking and her mouth snapped shut.

Alice turned away from the tank. She looked around the dark room. Then she smiled again. This smile was huge, but it didn't look very happy.

"Let's step outside," she said. "We should check on your teacher. She looked pale."

Mrs. Goolsby had looked pale. But Malcolm didn't think that was the problem.

"Where's the snake?" he asked.

"In here, of course, silly," Alice said. Her smile was still in place.

"But where?" Dandy asked.

The rest of the class repeated Dandy's question. Alice's eyes darted around the room. "I'm not sure. Loose maybe."

The class screamed and raced for the door. Malcolm and Dandy were in the lead. Malcolm saw something rear up from the floor in front of them. It was long and skinny. It swayed back and forth. Then it spread a hood and hissed.

Malcolm tried to stop. But not everyone had seen the snake yet. They shoved him from behind. The force knocked him onto the ground right in front of Rex.

Chapter 3
Bug Spray Hero

As Malcolm hit the ground, Rex jumped backward. The snake seemed as surprised as Malcolm.

"Don't move," Alice squeaked behind Malcolm. "You should be fine as long as you don't scare Rex."

Scare Rex? Malcolm wasn't a chicken. He had stared down ghosts and monsters. But as he looked into Rex's face, he was shaking. Rex didn't look scared at all. He looked scary.

Rex swayed back and forth in front of Malcolm. Back, forth, back, forth. Malcolm felt a little dizzy. He began to sway, too. Back. Forth.

Rex lowered his hood and leaned slowly forward. Malcolm really didn't want the snake any closer.

"Don't move," Alice whispered. "Don't scare him."

Malcolm gritted his teeth, but he didn't move.

Closer and closer. The snake's tongue flicked out and touched Malcolm's nose. The tongue zipped back into his mouth. Then the snake jumped back again and slithered into the shadows.

Malcolm scrambled to his feet.

"Wow," Dandy said. "You must taste awful."

Malcolm rubbed at his nose. It was still slimy with sweat and bug spray. "He probably didn't like the bug spray."

"See?" Dandy grinned. "I knew you'd be glad I sprayed you."

"Everyone outside," Alice said. Her smile still wobbled. "I'll call someone to come and pop Rex back in his cage."

His classmates rushed for the door. Malcolm fell into step with Alice. "Do animals get out of their cages a lot here?"

"No, of course not," she said. "Not a lot."

"But sometimes?"

Alice shook her head. "Well, Rex has never gotten out of his cage before."

She pulled the shed door open. Malcolm could tell she had a lot of things she didn't want to tell him. She herded Malcolm and Dandy out into the sunshine.

Dandy poked around in his bag until he grabbed the bug spray. He squirted a glob on his hand and rubbed it in.

"Just in case there are more snakes. You can never be too careful," Dandy said.

The rest of the class crowded around Mrs. Goolsby. She looked even paler as the class told her about Rex.

"Are you okay?" she asked Malcolm.

Malcolm nodded.

"I saved the day with bug spray!" Dandy yelled.

"Oh. Well, good for you, Dandy," Mrs. Goolsby said. "Let's get away. I mean, let's move on to the next exhibit."

"Yes!" Alice said. "On to the monkeys."

"Monkeys!" The class cheered and trotted after Alice.

Malcolm pulled Dandy aside. He whispered, "Something is going on here."

Dandy agreed. "Why is no one talking about how I saved the day with bug spray?"

"You're talking about it plenty," Malcolm said.

Dandy crossed his arms and stuck out his lip. "It would still be better if other people talked about it."

"I'll try to fit it in my next conversation," Malcolm said. "But I think this park might have a bigger problem. I think animals get out of their cages a lot here."

Dandy frowned. "Alice said Rex had never gotten out before."

"Yeah, Rex has never gotten out before. I wonder who has."

Dandy shivered and looked around. "You think there might be other snakes loose out here?"

"I don't know what might be loose out here. We better stay on our toes."

Dandy stretched up onto his toes. "Fine. But I'm not sure I can run very fast this way, Malcolm."

Their class followed Alice down one of the trails. Malcolm just sighed and pulled Dandy along.

Chapter 4
Simon See, Simon Do

Alice led the group to a tall cage filled with swings, toys, and plants. They crowded around the monkey exhibit. Dandy and Malcolm squeezed into a spot near the cage door.

"Wow." Dandy looked up at the top of the enclosure. "That's bigger than my house."

Mrs. Goolsby pushed her glasses up on her nose. "Is that a baby monkey I see in there?" The baby monkey swung from

branch to branch. Then it hopped up onto a high platform in the cage.

Alice clapped her hands to get everyone's attention. "Yes, that's Simon. As you can see, we have a large family of howler monkeys. Police discovered them living in a tiny mobile home. Simon and his family are much happier here. They have lots of room and fresh air."

"Why is he up there?" Dandy asked, pointing to the platform.

"That's where his mother built her nest. Howlers are one of the few nest building monkeys."

Simon peered at them over the side of the platform. He jumped off to land on one of the bigger monkeys. The big monkey held an egg. Simon tried to grab it, but the big monkey pushed him away.

"Monkeys don't lay eggs," Dandy said. The baby monkey finally jumped away.

"No," Alice said. "The eggs are special treats. But don't stare at him while he eats. The adults can be grumpy about that."

But the warning came too late. The monkey had noticed Dandy pointing and staring. He glared at Dandy. Dandy smiled back. The monkey pulled back his arm and flung the egg.

Splat! It smacked Dandy in the middle of the forehead. Egg shells and goo dripped down his face. The rest of the class laughed.

Egg dripped from Dandy's face. Simon swung over to cling to the bars on the cage door. Malcolm was pretty sure the little monkey was laughing too.

Simon shook the door. The door sprung open.

Alice yelled for the kids to back away from the cage. The little monkey jumped from the swinging door. He landed right on top of Dandy's head.

"Hey, little guy!" Dandy reached up, and the monkey held onto his finger.

"Uh-oh," Malcolm muttered.

Dandy laughed as the baby monkey pulled his finger. "It's okay. Simon just wants to be friends."

Malcolm swallowed with a gulp and pointed. "Simon might, but I don't think they do."

The big monkeys howled. They pushed each other to get out through the open door. They were all looking at Dandy.

Dandy screamed and ran. The little monkey clung to his head, whooping.

Dandy waved his arms and raced down the path. "Help! Help!" The rest of their class ran with him.

The bigger monkeys raced after Dandy and Simon. They ran right by Malcolm without even looking at him.

The heavy cage door swung shut after the last monkey was gone. Malcolm frowned. What made the door open? And what made it shut?

Malcolm turned to look for Dandy. Alice and the other zookeepers joined the chase. Some of them had big nets to catch the monkeys.

"There's not much I can do there," Malcolm muttered. "But there might be something I can do here."

Malcolm opened his bag. He grabbed the Ecto-Handheld-Automatic-Heat-Sensitive-Laser-Enhanced Specter Detector. He turned it on and pointed it at the monkey cage door.

Bleep, bleep, bleep, bleep.

With the specter detector, Malcolm didn't have to guess what opened the cage. He could see.

A short, round man in a zoo uniform floated next to the door. But he wasn't looking at Malcolm. Instead, he peered inside the cage where three monkeys swung on the branches.

But these weren't howler monkeys. They were ghost monkeys!

"Hey," Malcolm said. "What do you think you're doing?"

The ghost turned to look at Malcolm. "I'm doing my job, kid."

Malcolm reached into his backpack. "Not anymore."

He pulled out the Ecto-Handheld-Automatic-Heat-Sensitive-Laser-Enhanced Ghost Zapper. It looked a lot like Dandy's bug spray. But this one zapped things that bugged Malcolm a lot more.

Malcolm held it up, pointing it at the ghost.

"What do you think you're doing?" the ghost demanded.

Malcolm smiled. "My job."

Chapter 5
Banned for Life

Malcolm didn't squeeze the trigger. Instead, he heard Dandy running up behind him. Malcolm turned as Simon leaped from Dandy's head. The monkey snatched the zapper out of his hand.

"Hey!" Malcolm yelled. "Give that back."

Simon jumped onto the outside of the monkey cage. He still had the ghost zapper in his hand. He scurried up the side.

The ghost zookeeper pointed at Malcolm and laughed. "Good job, kid!"

"I'll get around to you," Malcolm said.

He turned off the specter detector and shoved it into his backpack. Then he jumped onto the cage and started climbing. He had to get his ghost zapper back.

Simon perched on the very top of the monkey cage. He turned the ghost zapper over in his hands as he looked at it.

"Come here, Simon," Malcolm called.

The little monkey looked down at him. Simon stuck out his tongue.

"Give that back!" Malcolm yelled.

Simon just shook the ghost zapper at him. A blast of purple goo shot out of the zapper. It splattered all over Malcolm. Goo ran down his hair and face.

"Malcolm! Come down here at once!"

Malcolm definitely recognized that voice. It was Mrs. Goolsby.

He looked at her and noticed two things. First, she looked really mad. Second, she looked really small. He hadn't realized how high he'd climbed. He was halfway up the cage. The ground was far, far below.

Malcolm gulped. He really didn't want to climb any higher. But he had to get the zapper.

He forced himself to look up at Simon. The little monkey was back to shaking the ghost zapper.

Malcolm gritted his teeth and climbed. Simon looked down at him again. He grinned, showing off sharp little teeth.

The monkey held up the ghost zapper and pulled the trigger. Purple goo shot out, but the monkey was holding the ghost zapper backward. The goo sprayed him right in the face.

Simon jumped and dropped the ghost zapper. It rolled along one of the metal bars. Malcolm scrambled up faster in hopes of grabbing it.

He stretched, reaching out as far as he could. The ends of his fingers touched the ghost zapper. But it slipped between the bars and fell into the cage.

"No!" Malcolm yelled.

That's when two zookeepers grabbed the back of Malcolm's shirt. A third snagged Simon in a net.

"I have to get in the cage!" Malcolm yelled. The zookeepers climbed down the cage with Malcolm between them.

"Sorry kid," one of the zookeepers said. "But you're not a monkey."

"Simon dropped something of mine inside the cage," Malcolm said.

"I saw that!" Alice shouted. "I can't believe you gave the monkey bug spray. Don't you know that's dangerous? Shame on you!"

The zookeepers dumped Malcolm on the ground in front of Alice. He didn't know what to say. If he told her about the ghost zapper, she wouldn't believe him.

He hung his head. "It was an accident. The monkey grabbed it."

"And did you accidentally climb up the cage?" Alice asked.

"I was worried about Simon," Malcolm said. "With the dangerous bug spray."

Alice called to the zookeeper holding Simon. "Find that spray before you put the monkeys back in the cage."

Mrs. Goolsby and her class tromped back to the monkey cage. Alice frowned at

the teacher. The other zookeepers stood on either side of her, glaring.

"We're going to have to close the park for today. We need to catch the loose monkeys," Alice said. "I'm afraid you and your class will have to leave."

"But I didn't see the lions!" Rosie Main whined. "Or the tiger or the bears."

"Oh my," Mrs. Goolsby said. "But we need to stay safe."

"I need my, um, bug spray," Malcolm said.

"Dandy's mother will simply have to buy a new one," Mrs. Goolsby snapped.

Alice turned to her. "We can't have kids climbing the cages. This young man is banned from the park. Banned for life!"

Chapter 6
Blame Rain

A paper ball bounced off of Malcolm's head. It landed on the floor of the school bus. It joined the other paper wads rolling around as the bus rumbled along. Malcolm slumped lower in the seat.

"Don't worry," Dandy said. "Everyone will forget all about this. Someday."

"It's not fair," Malcolm grumbled. "I didn't make the monkey steal my ghost zapper. And I couldn't let him keep it. It's valuable Ghost Detecting equipment."

Dandy swatted away another ball of paper. "I know."

"And they didn't throw us out because of me anyway," Malcolm said. He spoke louder so the other kids could hear him. "I didn't let the monkeys out of their cage."

Another wad of paper landed on his head.

Dandy brushed it off onto the floor. "I don't think they care."

"The ghost let the monkeys out," Malcolm whispered. "I saw him."

"What kind of ghost?" Dandy asked.

"A zookeeper, I think. The cage was full of ghost monkeys. I'm telling you, that park is haunted, big time. We have to do something about it."

"I don't know how we're going to do that," Dandy said. "You're banned for life, Malcolm. Plus, it's too far to ride our bikes out there."

"Maybe my dad would drive us," Malcolm said.

"Not if Mrs. Goolsby tells him you're banned for life."

"She might forget to tell him," Malcolm suggested.

"Sure," Dandy said. "You're doomed, dude."

Back at school, Mrs. Goolsby's class clumped to the room. She passed out math work sheets. "We can make good use of our extra time," she said, "with some division practice."

Other than Dandy, every single kid glared at Malcolm. Rosie Main even stuck out her tongue.

He glared back. *It wasn't my fault!*

When the final bell rang, kids rushed to the door. Even Mrs. Goolsby couldn't slow them down. Everyone wanted to see an end to the horrible day. Malcolm grabbed his backpack and started to follow.

"Malcolm!" Mrs. Goolsby said. "Come here, please."

Malcolm and Dandy exchanged a look.

"Good luck," Dandy whispered. Then he ran out the door.

With a sigh, Malcolm headed for the teacher's desk. She handed him a note. "Please give this to your parents."

He looked down at the folded paper. "It wasn't my fault."

"Oh?" Mrs. Goolsby said. "Did someone make you climb the cage to retrieve Dandy's bug spray?"

Malcolm looked up at the teacher. She was the one grown-up at school who might believe him. Mrs. Goolsby knew that ghosts could be real.

"It wasn't bug spray," he whispered. "It was my ghost zapper."

Her eyes widened. "Ghost zapper!"

"I saw a ghost in a zookeeper's uniform," Malcolm said. "I think he let the monkeys

out. Maybe the snake too. And if he did, who knows what he might let out next? Maybe a lion or a tiger or a bear."

"Oh my," Mrs. Goolsby said.

"I had to try to get the ghost zapper back," Malcolm insisted. "I was trying to save everyone."

Mrs. Goolsby looked at him for a long moment. Then she took the note back. Malcolm brightened, but Mrs. Goolsby shook her finger at him.

"What you did was dangerous. Even with a good reason, you shouldn't have climbed the cage. But I will think about everything a little longer before I decide how best to tell your parents."

Gloom smacked Malcolm like a rain of paper wads. Could his day get any worse?

Chapter 7
Unexpected Help

After Malcolm met Dandy in the hall, the boys went to Malcolm's house. They headed to his basement lab. For once, Malcolm beat Dandy to the beanbag chair. He moaned. "Everyone hates me."

"Not everyone. I like you." Dandy pulled the specter detector out of Malcolm's bag. "And I know someone else." He powered on the specter detector. *Bleep, bleep.*

Malcolm's ghost dog appeared and danced around Malcolm's legs. *Yip! Yip!*

"Hi Spooky," Malcolm said. "It's too bad you couldn't come to the zoo with us. You would have liked the ghost monkeys."

Yip! Yip!

Malcolm slumped deeper in the chair. "This was the worst day ever."

"At least Mrs. Goolsby didn't make you take the note home," Dandy said.

"That's true." Malcolm guessed the day could have been much worse. He could be banned for life and grounded forever.

"Malcolm!" Mom's voice boomed down the steps from the kitchen.

Malcolm jumped up. "Coming!"

"Your mom sounds mad," Dandy said. "Maybe I should wait here."

"Chicken."

Malcolm ran up the stairs. His mom stood in the middle of the kitchen. She had

her hands on her hips. Cocoa leaned against a counter and smirked. Her purple lip gloss reminded Malcolm of the ghost zapper goo.

"Is it true?" Mom asked. "Did you open the door to the monkey cage today?"

"No!" Malcolm said.

"That's not what I heard," Cocoa sang.

"Cocoa," Mom said. "Let me handle this."

Cocoa didn't say anything else. Instead, she made faces from the doorway.

"I did not open the monkey cage!" Malcolm insisted. "Honest, Mom, I didn't. Mrs. Goolsby would even tell you I didn't."

Mom looked at him for a long moment. "But someone did? You had to leave the zoo early."

Malcolm nodded eagerly. "The zoo is having trouble with their cages. The

animals keep getting out. That's why they sent us home."

Mom relaxed a little. "Oh, well, that's too bad. I know you were looking forward to the field trip."

Cocoa waved her hands in the air. "You don't believe him, do you? Ask him about being banned for life."

Before Mom could ask, the doorbell rang. Mom gave Cocoa and Malcolm one of her looks. "We'll get back to this."

"You're in so much trouble," Cocoa whispered.

"Yeah, right." Malcolm walked right by her. He wasn't going to let her see him sweat.

He followed Mom to the front door. And gasped.

His day really could get worse.

"Hello, Mrs. Goolsby. What a surprise." Mom gave him a questioning glance. Malcolm didn't know what to say. Had Mrs. Goolsby decided to deliver the note in person?

"I wanted to talk to Malcolm about a special project," Mrs. Goolsby said. "He and Dandy were so interested in the zoo today. They do love to be helpful."

"A special project? How wonderful." Mom beamed. "Do come in. Can I get you something?"

"I would love a glass of water," Mrs. Goolsby said. She turned her smile toward Malcolm. "Is Dandy here too?"

Malcolm bobbed his head. "Yeah. He's downstairs in my lab."

Mom laughed nervously. "Malcolm likes to pretend the basement's a lab."

"Maybe I can explain the project to you there," Mrs. Goolsby said.

Malcolm didn't know what his teacher had in mind. But she hadn't told Mom about being banned from the zoo. Mom was so happy now. She would never believe Cocoa's gossip.

He led Mrs. Goolsby down to the lab. Dandy was sitting in the beanbag chair. He stuck out his leg for Spooky to jump over.

"Oh my!" Mrs. Goolsby said. "Is that a ghost?"

"It's my ghost dog, Spooky." Malcolm patted Spooky's head. *Yip! Yip!*

"I never imagined animals could have ghosts."

"You should have seen the ghost monkeys," Malcolm said. "The monkey cage was full of them."

Mrs. Goolsby knelt down and Spooky raced over to dance around her. She smiled at the ghost dog. "I've been thinking about what you said. About the ghost zookeeper letting animals out of their cages. Someone needs to stop him."

"No one even sees him," Malcolm said.

"You did," Mrs. Goolsby said. "I think it might be up to us to stop him."

Malcolm blinked at her. "Us?"

She nodded. "Unless you two have learned to drive, I think you need me. I've already told your mom about a special project. We're taking another trip to the Wild Wonderland Animal Rescue. I'll drive."

"They won't let me in," Malcolm said. "I'm banned for life, remember?"

"I can help with that."

They turned to the bottom of the stairs. Grandma Eunice stood on the steps.

Malcolm gasped. "You walked down the stairs?"

Malcolm's great-grandmother always used her wheelchair around the house. She

pretended to be weak and loony most of the time. She said it's what his mom expected. And it kept her from doing chores. Malcolm thought that was brilliant.

"I had to hear what was going on," Grandma Eunice said. "We have to make this quick before Cocoa sees me." She introduced herself to Mrs. Goolsby and they shook hands.

"How are you going to get the zoo to let me in?" Malcolm asked.

"With a disguise!"

Chapter 8
Undercover Detector

Dandy showed up early the next morning. He wanted to watch Malcolm try on disguises. They had to be ready before Mrs. Goolsby arrived. She was taking them back to Wild Wonderland Animal Rescue.

Malcolm stared at himself in the mirror in Grandma Eunice's room. He'd been trying on weird things for over an hour.

Instead of his normal hair, he had blond curls. And his eyes were huge. He blinked

behind big, round glasses that made everything blurry. But the worst part of the disguise was the shoes. "I'm not sure I can walk in these."

Grandma Eunice nodded. "They do take some practice, but they'll make you much taller."

"Why do I need to be taller?" Malcolm asked.

"Simple," Grandma Eunice said. "Because the kid they banned for life is a shrimp."

"Hey!" Malcolm complained.

"Sorry, kiddo," Grandma Eunice said. "You inherited shortness from me. It's too bad you didn't get my singing voice instead. Or my fashion flair."

"Right." Malcolm looked down at his feet again. Grandma Eunice had given

him blue high-top sneakers printed with eyeballs. They also had three-inch thick soles. Malcolm felt like he was on stilts.

"Why do you have these anyway?"

"I wanted to be taller so I could see the board better on bingo night. And the blue matches my eyes." She sighed. "But I forgot we sit during bingo. They didn't help."

"Do I get a disguise too?" Dandy asked.

"You weren't banned, Dandy," Malcolm pointed out.

"I could have been. I ran away with a monkey. I still might need a disguise."

"How about a wig?" Grandma Eunice asked. "I have a lot of them." She pointed at her bed. Wigs lay in furry piles like brightly colored puppies.

Dandy picked up one of the wigs. He plunked it on his head.

Malcolm looked him over. "You look like you have an animal on your head again."

"I like it," Grandma Eunice said. "The purple matches your shirt."

Dandy walked over to peer at himself in the mirror. The purple curls on his head drooped down over one eye. "I do like purple."

Malcolm looked at them side by side in the mirror. They looked like two blurry clowns. They were supposed to be sneaking into the zoo in disguises. He didn't think they should stand out.

Mrs. Goolsby walked into Grandma Eunice's room then. She took one glance at Malcolm and Dandy and frowned. "The boys might be a little too attention getting."

"That's what I was trying for," Grandma Eunice explained. "No one would suspect

them of trying to sneak in when they look like that."

"I suppose that's right," Mrs. Goolsby said. "We don't have time to change anyway. We should get to the park early. There won't be so many people around."

"Great," Grandma Eunice said. "Let me get my hat."

The teacher blinked her eyes several times. "Excuse me?"

"I'm coming too," Grandma Eunice said.

"I don't think so," Mrs. Goolsby said.

Grandma Eunice leaned forward in her wheelchair. "I'm a Ghost Detector too."

Malcolm groaned.

"Fine," Grandma Eunice said with a huff. "I'm support staff." Then she pointed at Mrs. Goolsby. "But I intend to look after my great-grandson."

Mrs. Goolsby put up her hands. "Fine. We better get going."

"Yippee!" Grandma Eunice cheered as she rolled her chair out of the room. "I call front seat!"

"Right," Malcolm muttered. He hefted his backpack onto his shoulder. "There's no way this can go wrong."

Chapter 9
Ice Cream & Monkeys

Grandma Eunice was right about one thing. No one at the park recognized Malcolm. Not even when they trooped by Alice. But everyone stared at them. It was going to be hard to sneak around and catch the ghost.

Mrs. Goolsby led the group through the zoo. She pushed Grandma Eunice's wheelchair to a food and gift shop area. "Stay here. I'll talk to Alice. Maybe she'll give me the 'bug spray' we lost."

Then Mrs. Goolsby left. Grandma Eunice pushed her chair to the nearest food stand. She began ordering snacks. Lots of snacks. "Do we need all that?" Malcolm asked.

"It's part of the disguise," she whispered. "No one looks sneaky with ice cream."

"That sounds right to me," Dandy agreed.

Malcolm rolled his eyes. "You just want ice cream."

Dandy nodded. "That too."

Malcolm walked over to the bushes beside the gift shop. He turned on the specter detector in his backpack. *Bleep, bleep. Bleep, bleep. Bleep, bleep, bleep, bleep.*

"Dandy," he whispered. "Hey Dandy!"

His friend peered into the bushes. Dandy lapped at a three-scoop ice cream cone. Another cone dripped onto his hand. "Did you lose something in the bushes?"

"No. There's a ghost nearby."

"I don't see anything, but here's your ice cream." Dandy held out the drippy cone.

Malcolm reached out to take the ice cream. Then a hairy arm darted out of the bushes. This one snatched the cone. The arm smooshed it down on top of Dandy's head.

"What did you do that for?" Dandy pouted as the treat dripped off his nose.

"I didn't," Malcolm said. "But I found a ghost."

"Where?"

A ghost monkey floated out of the bushes. It grabbed Dandy's other cone and smashed it on Malcolm's head. The monkey howled with laughter.

"Right there," Malcolm said. "Now if I just had my ghost zapper."

Suddenly a huge net swooshed down over the ghost monkey. "Gotcha!"

The ghost zookeeper looked at Malcolm and Dandy. "Excuse me, boys. I need to get this one into the monkey cage."

Malcolm couldn't believe it. Two ghosts and no ghost zapper. "You better not open that monkey cage again," he said.

"I have to," the ghost said. "I have to keep these guys safe. It's my job. It's what Wild Wonderland Animal Rescue is all about."

"But you're making the park dangerous for everyone!" Malcolm insisted.

For a moment, the ghost looked upset. Then he shook his head. "Don't be silly. I have to take this guy to his home."

Malcolm watched the ghost float away with his big net. He didn't have his ghost zapper. But he had to do something!

Malcolm and Dandy raced after the ghost.

"Wait for me!" Grandma Eunice yelled.

"Get the ghost zapper," Malcolm yelled back. He looked at the specter detector in his backpack. It was still on.

As they ran, ghost animals appeared in every cage they passed. A ghost giraffe trailed along behind two live giraffes. A ghost lion napped on a rock. A flock of ghost pigeons sat on the park's elephant fountain.

The zoo was full of ghosts!

Chapter 10
A Place for Ghosts

The ghost zookeeper stopped next to the monkey cage. Inside, live monkeys perched on branches next to ghost monkeys.

"Don't open that door," Malcolm yelled. "You'll let the monkeys out."

"Don't be silly," the zookeeper said. "I'm a professional."

The door of the cage swung open. Ghost monkeys and live monkeys rushed toward it. "Oh my!" the zookeeper said. He shoved the ghost monkey into the cage.

Malcolm and Dandy slammed the door shut. The monkeys couldn't get out. They threw leaves, sticks, and mushy fruit at the boys through the bars.

"You have to stop doing this," Malcolm said. He wiped bananas from his face.

"But ghost animals need homes too," the zookeeper said. "And Wild Wonderland Animal Rescue has always been that home."

"This is a home for live animals," Malcolm insisted. "You need a different place for ghost animals."

"There is no place," the zookeeper said.

"There could be."

Malcolm, Dandy, and the ghost turned. Mrs. Goolsby pushed Grandma Eunice's wheelchair over to them. "You could move the ghosts to the Super Funtime Zoo. No one uses it anymore," the teacher said.

The zookeeper frowned. "No! That was a terrible place. It was too noisy and too crowded. The animals were miserable."

"They don't have to be," Malcolm said. "There aren't any people there anymore. The animals wouldn't even need to be in cages. Think how much fun the monkeys could have swinging on that roller coaster."

The ghost monkeys crowded next to the cage door. They hooted eagerly.

"That might work," the zookeeper said. "It has been hard to keep them in the cages." Then he whispered, "Once they figure out they can go through the bars."

The ghost monkeys slipped out of the cage. One threw an arm around Dandy. Another played with Malcolm's bag. A third snatched Malcolm's wig and plunked it on his own head.

"We need to get them to the zoo fast," Malcolm said.

"But how?" Mrs. Goolsby asked. "They won't fit in my car."

"It's not far," Grandma Eunice added. "They could walk. We can have a parade!"

"Yay!" Dandy jumped up and down. "I love parades." The ghost monkeys jumped up and down with him, hooting.

"We can try," the ghost zookeeper said. "Let's go!"

They made a very strange parade as they wove through the zoo. At every cage, the zookeeper called. Then ghost animals poured out to join the group. The parade grew more and more crowded.

Malcolm kept the specter detector on. They had to be sure to get every animal. That meant everyone could see the ghosts.

A ghost lion roared at a group of kids. The kids roared back. Then their parents grabbed them and ran out of the park. A ghost tiger chased them. But the zookeeper called it back.

When they passed the reptile house, a ghost snake slithered by Mrs. Goolsby. She whimpered. The zookeeper gathered the snake in a net and bowed. She thanked him in a shaky voice.

Ghost birds landed on Grandma Eunice's chair. She threw popcorn to them. They couldn't eat it, but they enjoyed the effort.

Malcolm and Dandy marched ahead of the parade with the zookeeper. Suddenly, something snaked around Dandy's waist. He screamed.

Malcolm thought it was a ghost snake for a moment. Then he saw it was attached

to a huge head. The ghost elephant lifted Dandy onto his shoulders for a ride.

"This is great!" Dandy yelled. "You should come up here too!"

The ghost elephant lifted Malcolm up to sit beside Dandy. They marched through the rest of the zoo. Some people froze and stared as they walked by. Some ran away. But finally they reached the front entrance.

Alice stood next to the front gate. Her mouth fell open as she stared.

"I don't think you'll have anymore trouble with your cages, thanks to the Ghost Detectors!" Malcolm yelled to her.

Dandy waved at Alice, and she waved back. Her mouth was still open.

The ghost parade marched through the parking lot and down the road. Cars honked. Some just turned and raced away.

Malcolm twisted around to see the line of ghosts behind them.

Monkeys rode on the giraffes. They slid down their necks and scrambled back up. One monkey rode on the back of a camel. Lions and bears growled at each other.

Finally they reached Super Funtime Zoo and Theme Park. The fence was so rusty that the ghost elephants just pushed it over.

They marched across the cracked, weedy lot and into the park. The ghost zebras and antelopes raced down the broken paths. Ghost monkeys climbed into bumper cars and hooted. Ghost rams bumped the cars, pushing them around.

"They look so happy," the zookeeper said. He grinned at the boys as they slid down the elephant's trunk. "Thank you."

"Happy to help," Malcolm said. "Solving ghost problems is what we do best."

The zookeeper floated away to help a ghost turtle. It struggled to climb a fountain that still dribbled water into a slimy basin.

"I wish I'd gotten my ghost zapper back," Malcolm said. "I'll have to buy a new one. The old one cost me a month's allowance."

Mrs. Goolsby pushed Grandma Eunice's wheelchair up to them. "I can do something about that." She opened her big purse hanging on her shoulder. She pulled out the ghost zapper. "Alice gave it back."

Malcolm whooped as he took the ghost zapper. He would have hugged it, but he didn't want anyone to laugh. Still, he carefully slipped it into his backpack.

Mrs. Goolsby ducked as a ghost flamingo flew by. The ghost zookeeper ran in pursuit.

"Everyone's going to know ghosts are real now," she said.

Grandma Eunice laughed. "Maybe not."

"But there was a ghost parade!" Dandy said.

"Everyone saw them," Malcolm added.

Grandma Eunice laughed again and shook her head. "People believe what they want to believe. I've seen some weird stuff in my life. And no one believes me."

Malcolm had to agree with her on that. Grandma Eunice was always telling stories that no one believed.

Grandma Eunice grinned. "But that's okay. We know what's real. Now, I believe we could really use some ice cream."

That was an idea they could all agree on!

Questions for You

From Ghost Detectors
Malcolm and Dandy

Dandy: I love costumes and disguises. We should wear them more often. What's the wildest thing you've ever dressed up as?

Malcolm: It was weird when Mrs. Goolsby helped us with the ghosts, but she's the best teacher, ever. Who is your favorite teacher? Why?

Dandy: I think being a zookeeper would be a great job. They get to help animals and eat at the snack stands every day! What's your dream job?

Malcolm: I always wanted a pet monkey. But after visiting Wild Wonderland Animal Rescue, I think I'll stick with Cocoa. She throws stuff enough. What's your favorite animal? Why?

MAR 2 8 2018